Perrie
the Paramedic
Fairy

To Tamsyn and Jack

Special thanks to
Rachel Elliot

ORCHARD BOOKS

First published in Great Britain in 2015 by Orchard Books
This edition published in 2016 by The Watts Publishing Group

3 5 7 9 10 8 6 4 2

© 2016 Rainbow Magic Limited.
© 2016 HIT Entertainment Limited.
Illustrations © 2015 The Watts Publishing Group Ltd

HIT entertainment

The moral rights of the author and illustrator have been asserted.

A CIP catalogue record for this book is available from the British Library.

ISBN 978 1 40834 889 5

Printed in Great Britain

MIX
Paper from
responsible sources
FSC® C104740

FSC
www.fsc.org

The paper and board used in this book are made from wood from responsible sources

Orchard Books
An imprint of Hachette Children's Group
Part of The Watts Publishing Group Limited
Carmelite House, 50 Victoria Embankment, London EC4Y 0DZ

An Hachette UK Company
www.hachette.co.uk
www.hachettechildrens.co.uk

Perrie
the Paramedic
Fairy

by Daisy Meadows

ORCHARD

www.rainbowmagic.co.uk

Jack Frost's Spell

These silly helpful folk I see
Don't know they could be helping me.
But they will fail and I will smirk,
And let the goblins do the work.

I'll show this town I've got some nerve
And claim rewards that I deserve.
The prize on offer will be mine
And I will see the trophy shine!

Contents

Marathon Man

"I've never seen the park so busy," said Rachel Walker, gazing around.

It was a sunny spring morning, and Tippington Park was packed with people. Everyone was there to watch the start of the Tippington Town Half Marathon.

"I hope your dad wins," said Rachel's
best friend, Kirsty Tate.

Kirsty was staying with Rachel for
the spring half-term holidays. They
both looked across to where Mr Walker
was warming up for the race. He was
wearing a white vest top and running

trousers. The
number seven
was pinned to his
vest.

"He's in with
a good chance,"
said Rachel. "He's
been training
every day for
months! But he
always says it's not
about winning."

"It's about taking part," agreed Mrs Walker, who was standing behind them. "Your dad has already raised lots of money for charity."

The girls gazed around at the crowds of runners and spectators. Everyone looked happy and excited. The half-marathon was an important event for Tippington Town. People looked forward to it all year long.

"I wonder if we'll see any of our fairy friends today," said Rachel.

"Or any goblins,"
Kirsty added. "We
should keep our
eyes peeled – the
Tippington Helper
of the Year Award
is being presented
tomorrow and we still

need to find two of the Helping Fairies'
magical objects."

The nominations for the Tippington
Helper of the Year Award had been
announced at the start of the week. It
was a very important local prize that
recognised the special people in the
community whose job was to help others.
This year it was especially exciting for
Rachel and Kirsty, because Rachel's
Aunt Lesley was one of the nominees.

She was an excellent doctor, and the girls felt sure that she would win. But they were the only humans who knew that the award ceremony might go very wrong indeed.

Two days ago, Jack Frost had stolen the magical objects that belonged to the Helping Fairies. He had sent his goblins to the human world with the fairies' magical objects and ordered them to do the jobs of the award nominees. He wanted to take the credit for himself so he could win the award without actually helping anyone.

Kirsty and Rachel had already helped Martha the Doctor Fairy and Ariana the Firefighter Fairy to get their magical objects back, but there were still two left to find, and the ceremony was getting closer. The girls felt sure that Jack Frost and his goblins would be planning to cause as much trouble as possible for the award nominees.

"Do you think the goblins might be here?" asked Rachel.

"We know that they're hanging around Tippington to take over from the award nominees," said Kirsty. "There are bound to be some of the nominees here today. I bet the goblins won't be far away."

They looked around, but for now, everything seemed calm and goblin-free. Then they saw Aunt Lesley coming out of the first-aid station. It looked peaceful and the ambulance beside the station was standing quiet. Aunt Lesley spotted the girls and came over to join them beside the track, smiling.

"Good morning, girls!" she said. "I've come to cheer for your dad, Rachel."

Mr Walker was just coming over to join them, and he heard what she said.

"Thanks, Lesley," he said with a grin. "It's helpful to know I've got so much support – it makes me determined to run my fastest!"

Just then a loudspeaker crackled.

"Would all runners please make their way to the starting line?" said a loud, echoing voice. "The race is about to start."

Mr Walker hugged the girls and then headed over to join the other competitors.

"Good luck!" called Rachel, Kirsty, Mrs Walker and Aunt Lesley.

There were so many people crowding around that it was hard to see the person who was starting the race. But they heard the crack of a starting pistol. A huge cheer went up as the runners surged forward.

"They're off!" shouted Rachel, jumping up and down in excitement. "Go on, Dad, you can do it!"

Paramedics in a Panic

The girls and Aunt Lesley cheered loudly as Mr Walker ran past them.

"I guess you girls are waiting here to see the end of the race?" asked Aunt Lesley.

Rachel and Kirsty nodded.

"Are you going to wait with us?" Rachel asked. "We could get ice creams

— Mum said that there are usually lots of food stalls around."

"I'd love to, but my patients need me," said Aunt Lesley. "I have to hurry back to my surgery."

"No wonder your patients love you," said Kirsty. "You're very dedicated to them."

"You're bound to win Tippington Helper of the Year!" Rachel added.

"There are lots of people who help others in Tippington," smiled Aunt Lesley, glancing over at the first-aid station. "My friends the paramedics, for example."

"What do they do?" Kirsty asked.

"They work on board ambulances and give people first aid to make them feel better," Aunt Lesley replied. "They're

here today to look
after any runners
who might get
injured during
the race. They
have to think
and act fast,
because people
are depending
on them. In
fact, the senior
paramedic has been
nominated for the Tippington Helper of
the Year Award, just like me."

The girls glanced at each other. If the
goblins were nearby, they would certainly
be somewhere close to an award
nominee. They had to find a way to get
closer to the first-aid station.

"Aunt Lesley, might you have time to introduce us to the paramedics before you go to work?" Rachel asked. "We'd love to find out more about what they do."

Aunt Lesley looked at her watch and smiled.

"I've got five minutes," she said. "I'm so pleased that you both want to know more about helping jobs. I enjoy my work very much, and I know that the paramedics do too."

She led the girls to the first-aid station and walked up to the man and woman wearing dark-green uniforms. They were checking their supplies when the girls arrived.

"Colin and Tiana, this is my niece Rachel and her friend Kirsty," said Aunt Lesley. "Girls, Colin is the senior paramedic I was telling you about."

"Welcome!" said Colin with a friendly smile. "Would you like to see the inside of our ambulance?"

"Ooh, yes please!" said Rachel and Kirsty together.

"I must go," said Aunt Lesley. "I'll leave you in Colin and Tiana's capable hands."

They said goodbye to Aunt Lesley and then Tiana and Colin led them into the ambulance.

"There are so many machines!" said Kirsty, gazing around in wonder. There were dials, switches and screens everywhere she looked.

"We've got equipment for almost every sort of injury," said Tiana. "This is a heart monitor, and this is oxygen for people who are having trouble breathing."

"What's in all your little cupboards?" asked Rachel, looking at the cubbyholes above and around the trolley bed.

"All our medical kits are stored in there, with things like bandages, plasters, slings and gauze," said Colin. "It's also where we keep back-up supplies, in case we run out of anything."

He showed them a blood-pressure cuff and an inflatable splint.

He had just picked up a spinal collar when they heard someone calling for help outside the ambulance. They all hurried out and saw one of the runners standing outside the first-aid station, holding her knee.

"Are you OK?" asked Kirsty, hurrying over to her.

"What happened?" asked Rachel.

"I tripped over a stone and grazed my knee," said the woman, wincing in pain. "If

I can get it treated quickly, I can still join the race."

Rachel and Kirsty looked around, but to their surprise Colin and Tiana were still standing beside the ambulance. They weren't even looking at the injured woman.

"Colin?" called Kirsty. "This lady needs some help."

She expected him to dash over to her at once, but Colin glanced at the woman's knee and then looked away again. He had turned rather green in the face, and he looked as if he might be sick.

"I can't bear to look," he said.
"Suddenly the sight of blood makes me
feel ill."

"Tiana, can you help?" Rachel asked.

"Oh my goodness, it's an emergency!"
cried Tiana, opening her eyes very wide.
"We have to do something! I can't
remember how to treat a graze! Where's
the kit? How do I start?"

She was panting
and getting very
red in the face.
Then she burst
into tears, sat
down and put
her head in her
hands.

"She's panicking,"
said the runner,

sounding confused. "That's not very helpful."

Rachel and Kirsty exchanged a quick, worried glance. Paramedics should be quick-thinking and calm in an emergency, and they certainly shouldn't turn green at the sight of blood!

"I'm sure Colin and Tiana are acting strangely because Jack Frost has taken the Helping Fairies' magical objects," said Kirsty in a low voice. "It's so unfair. He wants to be Helper of the Year without actually helping anybody, and he's spoiling things for everyone else."

"We have to try to get Colin and Tiana back to normal," said Rachel. "But first, let's help this poor lady. I know what to do about a grazed knee – I've had so many of them!"

"Me too," said Kirsty with a smile. "I'll go and get the medical kit from the ambulance – I remember where Colin and Tiana keep it."

While Tiana groaned and Colin leaned against the side of the ambulance, Kirsty fetched a small medical kit. Rachel used a sterile wipe to clean the graze. Then Kirsty gently put some antiseptic cream onto the woman's knee.

"Now we just need a plaster," she said. "Look — it's the last one in the kit."

As soon as the plaster was on her knee, the woman thanked them and sprinted off to join the race.

"Let's put some more plasters in the kit," said Rachel. "I saw a box in the ambulance earlier."

Colin and Tiana were still recovering from their shock, so the girls jumped into the ambulance and went over to the cupboard where they had seen the plasters. Kirsty took out the box. As she opened it, Perrie the Paramedic Fairy fluttered out!

A Help or a Hindrance?

"Hello, Perrie!" exclaimed Rachel. "Have you come to see the marathon?"

"No," said Perrie with panic in her voice. "Oh girls, please will you come and help me? Jack Frost is causing havoc!"

Before the girls could reply, they heard voices outside the ambulance.

Kirsty peeped out and saw that two
more people had arrived at the first aid
station – a little boy with a nosebleed
and a runner holding his side. Colin had
screwed up his eyes so he didn't have to
look at the blood, and Tiana had buried
her head in her hands as if it was all too
much for her.

"He looks as if he's got a stitch," said
Rachel, coming to stand beside Kirsty.
"Oh dear, they both need our help. The
paramedics don't know what to do."

"That's because Jack Frost still has
my magical flashing siren," said Perrie.
"The best way to help them is to come
with me. Don't forget, time in the
human world stands still while you're in
Fairyland."

"Then let's go!" said Rachel at once.

"We can't let Jack Frost make any more trouble!"

"Oh, thank you!" Perrie exclaimed.

She waved her wand, and a long green ribbon twisted out of the tip. It coiled around the girls, tying itself into bows and rippling like a wave. Rachel and Kirsty shrank to fairy size, and beautiful wings carried them twirling into the air.

Then, in a sparkling burst of rainbow colours, they were whisked away to Fairyland.

With sparkles of fairy dust fading around them, Rachel and Kirsty found themselves standing among a group of toadstool houses. They could see the Fairyland Palace on the hill in the distance. As they looked around, the doors of the little houses opened and

a few curious fairies peeped out. The girls recognised some of them at once.

"Look, there's Francesca the Football Fairy!" exclaimed Kirsty. "Hi, Francesca! Oh, what's wrong with her poor foot?"

Francesca's right foot was in a plaster cast. They saw Bethany the Ballet Fairy with a bandaged toe and Alesha the Acrobat Fairy with a bandage on the top of her head. Then Bertram, the frog footman, hobbled past on crutches.

In fact, every single fairy they saw seemed to have some sort of injury.

"What's happened to everyone?" asked Rachel in a shocked voice. "Bertram, are you all right?"

Bertram smiled at her.

"We're all fine," he said. "No one is really hurt at all. But Jack Frost has been zooming around in an ambulance with the light flashing and the siren blaring. He's ordered his goblins to bandage everyone up, even though they're not injured."

"But why?" asked Kirsty.

"He's pretending to be helpful," said Perrie with a sigh. "He takes the credit for helping everyone, even though he isn't helping at all. He's just being a big hindrance! Francesca can't play football with a cast on her foot. Bethany can't dance and Alesha can't stand on her head."

"It's impossible for me to open doors while I've got these crutches," Bertram added. "I keep tripping people up."

"Jack Frost loves thinking of new ways to cause trouble," said Rachel. "We won't let him spoil things for everyone!"

"Wait," said Kirsty, putting her head on one side. "Can you hear something?"

They all listened. *NEE-NAW! NEE-NAW!* It was a siren, and it was growing louder and louder.

"It's Jack Frost," said Bertram with a groan. "He's coming back with his awful ambulance. Hide!"

As Bertram dived behind a rose bush,

an ice-blue ambulance came zooming
over the hill towards them. Its light
was flashing to show that there was an
emergency, and the girls could see that
Jack Frost was hunched over the steering
wheel. Five goblins were piled up in the
passenger seat, clinging on to each other
and looking terrified. Each goblin had
a big red cross painted on his knobbly
green forehead.

"He's going much too fast," said Kirsty
as the ambulance hurtled past. "I hope
he doesn't have an accident. It's lucky
his siren and light warned us that he was
coming."

"That's not his light," cried Perrie in a desperate voice. "It's my magical flashing siren!"

Siren in the Snow

"We have to help Perrie get her siren back," said Rachel, turning towards Kirsty.

But Kirsty was already fluttering into the air.

"Come on!" she exclaimed to her friends. "Let's chase them!"

Rachel and Perrie zoomed towards her, and the three fairies flew after the ambulance as fast as they could. They zipped over toadstool houses, up hills and down into daisy-strewn valleys. They were going so quickly that everything below looked blurry. The girls grinned at each other as they urged their wings to flap faster and faster. They zoomed towards the very edges of Fairyland, leaving the exquisite palace behind in the distance. Perrie took the lead, her blonde hair streaming out behind her as they flew.

"We've almost caught it up!" she cried.
"Keep going!"

When the ambulance reached an
extremely steep hill, it slowed down
slightly. Ice was sparkling on the road,
and they could see Jack Frost's castle
in the distance. The hills ahead were
glittering with snow and ice. Panting,
the fairies caught up with
the ambulance and
flew right above it,
trying to decide
what to do.

"Let's just swoop down and take the siren from the top of the ambulance," Rachel suggested.

Perrie shook her head. "It's going too fast," she said. "We need the ambulance to stop."

"I've got an idea!" said Kirsty. "Jack Frost might stop if he thinks there's a patient to treat. We just have to get ahead of the ambulance."

They all put on a burst of speed and passed the ambulance, flying over the hill so they were hidden from sight on the other side. Kirsty swooped down and landed on the steep, snowy hill.

"Stay high up so they can't see you!" she called to Rachel and Perrie. "I'll try to get the ambulance to stop."

Kirsty kneeled on the snowy ground and held one of her wings as if it were injured. She hung her head to pretend that she was crying. At that moment, the ambulance came hurtling over the brow of the hill.

"Help! Please stop!" Kirsty cried out, waving her arm.

The ambulance screeched to a halt and
the window was wound down.
Jack Frost's spiky head poked out and he
glared at her.

"What's the matter with you?" he
snapped.

"My wing needs to be bandaged," she
replied. "Can you help me?"

Jack Frost leaned across, opened the passenger door and then shoved the goblins out into the snow.

"Bandage her wing," he barked at them. "Do it now, so I get even more credit for being helpful! And hurry up – I want my lunch."

Complaining in loud voices, the goblins opened the back of the ambulance and clambered in to find their bandaging kit.

Meanwhile, Rachel fluttered carefully
down towards the magical flashing siren.
She reached out her hand towards it, but
just at that moment, Jack Frost turned it
on again. *NEE-NAW! NEE-NAW!*
Startled, Rachel
sprang back
and tumbled
off the
front
of the
ambulance.
As she
fluttered her
wings to stop
herself from falling,
she accidentally tumbled against the
windscreen. Turning in midair, she saw
Jack Frost's cold blue eyes glaring at her.

52

"Quickly, grab the siren!" Rachel yelled.

She flew up and Perrie dived towards it, but Jack Frost reached up one of his long arms and snatched it off the roof of the ambulance.

"I know exactly what you want!" he bawled at the top of his voice. "You're not getting this siren from me – I'm having way too much fun with it!"

Bruised Bottoms

"That siren belongs to Perrie," said Kirsty, jumping up. "Give it back to her right now!"

Jack Frost blew a big raspberry at her and then leaped out of the ambulance and started to run.

"Be careful!" Kirsty called after him.

"This hill is really steep and slippery —
you might fall and get hurt!"

"That sort of thing only happens to
weedy fairies," sneered Jack Frost with
an unpleasant laugh. "I'm so clever, I
can run as fast as I want and still not
fall over."

He sprinted off down the hill, and
the three fairies zoomed after him.
Behind them, the goblins started yelling
and wailing.

"Don't leave us behind!"

"Come back!"

"Slow down!" cried Rachel. "Be
careful!"

But Jack only laughed at all the
shouting and ran faster. He looked up to
check where the fairies were, and then
disaster struck! He slipped on a large

patch of ice and slid forwards down the steep hill, scrabbling and yelling. His arms whirled around like windmills and he squealed and screeched, but nothing could stop him.

"What can we do?" Kirsty called out.

Before they could think of a plan, Jack Frost struck a bump, flew into the air and landed on his bottom on a frozen puddle. CRACK! The ice broke and Jack Frost's bottom sank into the freezing water.

"YOWWWWCH!" he squealed,
struggling to his feet. "My poor bony
bottom! This is agony! I'm hurt! Call the
doctor! Call the air ambulance!"

He clutched his
bottom with one
hand and held on
to the siren with
the other. The
fairies hovered
in front of him.

"You can't be
too badly hurt
if you're able to
move around,"
said Perrie. "I
expect it's just a bruise."

"Just a bruise?" Jack Frost repeated in
outrage. "I'm probably scarred for life!"

Just then they heard a high-pitched screeching sound. The goblins were sliding down the hill and squealing at the tops of their voices. They hit the same bump, flew through the air and landed on Jack Frost. They all fell into a heap, arms and legs flailing around.

"My bottom!" cried one of the goblins. "Never mind *your* bottom, what about *my* bottom?" bellowed Jack Frost.

"Listen to me," said Rachel. "Please listen!"

But the goblins and Jack Frost were making so much noise that they didn't hear her. She took a deep breath and spoke in her loudest voice. "Perrie can make you all better!"

Everyone fell silent and stared at her.

"All you have to do is give her back the magical siren," Rachel went on.

At once, the goblins set up a loud clamour.

"Give it back! My bottom is throbbing!"

"Give it back! My arm hurts!"

"Give it back! Give it back!"

The Finishing Line

Faced by five glaring goblins, Jack Frost hesitated.

"Perrie is the only one who can help you," said Kirsty.

With a sigh and a frown, Jack Frost held out the siren and Perrie took it. A big smile spread across her face as she hugged the siren to her chest.

"Now you have to keep your end of the bargain," said Jack Frost.

"I *always* keep my promises," said Perrie.

She waved her wand over Jack Frost and the goblins. At once Jack Frost jumped to his feet, quickly followed by the goblins. But they didn't say thank you to Perrie. Jack Frost just glared at the fairies.

"You pesky fairies have spoiled everything again," he grumbled. "How am I supposed to win the Helper of the Year Award without the magical flashing siren?"

"Well, you helped by giving it back to
Perrie," said Rachel. "That's much more
helpful than bandaging people up when
there's nothing wrong with them."

Jack looked a bit less cross for a
moment. Then he turned, whipping
his cloak around him, and stamped off
through the snow. The goblins stumbled
after him, leaving a trail of large
footprints behind them.

"I'm so happy
we got the
siren back,"
said Perrie.
"I've been
very worried
about all the
paramedics.
Now everything
will get back to
normal."

She looked back at the ice-blue
ambulance at the top of the hill. Jack
Frost had forgotten about it now that he
didn't have the siren.

"The ambulance can't stay there," she
said.

She waved her wand and the
ambulance disappeared. Then Perrie

turned to Rachel and Kirsty and threw
her arms around them.

"You're both
amazing
friends," she
said with
a beaming
smile. "I
couldn't have
stopped Jack
Frost without
you. How can I
ever thank you enough?"

"We're just happy that we were
helpful," said Kirsty. "It feels good to
know that everything's back to normal."

"I wonder if Colin and Tiana will
be feeling better when we get back to
Tippington," Rachel said.

"You'll find out in a minute," Perrie replied. "It's time for me to send you home."

Rachel and Kirsty hugged the delighted fairy, and she waved her wand. The snow swirled around them and they closed their eyes. A few seconds later, they heard the distant chatter of a large crowd and found that they were back in the ambulance in Tippington Park.

"Rachel?" called Colin's voice. "Kirsty?"

The girls hurried out of the ambulance and saw Colin smiling at them. He was just closing his medical kit. Kirsty spotted the boy with the nosebleed walking away.

"Was he all right?" she asked.

"Oh yes," said Colin. "Just a little nosebleed – nothing to get upset about."

"So you don't mind the sight of blood?" Rachel asked.

Colin laughed. "I wouldn't be a very good paramedic if I were squeamish!"

Rachel and Kirsty shared a secret smile as Tiana came out of the first-aid station with the runner who had had a stitch. He thanked her and sprinted off, smiling.

"He's all better," said Tiana in a happy, calm voice. "Although the runners are starting to finish the race, so he'll have to be quick!"

Rachel glanced over to the track and saw Mr Walker running towards the finishing line.

"Dad's nearly finished!" she cried. "Come on, let's go and meet him!"

They said goodbye to Colin and Tiana, and then darted over to the finishing line. Mrs Walker was standing there, and she waved when she saw the girls.

"I've got a towel and a bottle of water ready for your dad," she said. "Do you want to give them to him?"

A few seconds later, Mr Walker
crossed the finishing line and saw
Rachel and Kirsty jumping up and down
in excitement.

"Hurray!" they both shouted. "You did
it! Hurray!"

Red in the face, laughing and puffing,
Mr Walker took the towel and the bottle
of water. He had a long drink and put
the towel around his neck.

"That's just what I needed," he said. "You're both wonderful helpers. Thank you!"

As Mrs Walker gave him a hug, Rachel and Kirsty smiled at each other.

"It's fun to help people," said Rachel.

"Especially the fairies," Kirsty agreed quietly. "And now there's only one more magical object to find."

"We just have to make sure we find it before tomorrow's Helper of the Year Award ceremony," said Rachel. "Do you think we can?"

Kirsty put her arm around her best friend's shoulders and gave her a squeeze.

"I *know* we can," she said. "The fairies are depending on us to help them, and we won't let them down!"

Meet the
Storybook Fairies

Can Rachel and Kirsty help get their new fairy friends'
magical objects back from Jack Frost, before all
their favourite stories are ruined?

www.rainbowmagicbooks.co.uk

Now it's time for Kirsty and
Rachel to help...

Lulu the Lifeguard Fairy

Read on for a sneak peek...

"Finally, I would like to thank my
wonderful patients, who have been kind
enough to nominate me for this award,"
said Aunt Lesley. "I look forward to
continuing to help them."

On the sofa in the Walker's sitting room,
Kirsty Tate and Rachel Walker clapped
with enthusiasm. Kirsty was visiting her
best friend for the spring half term, and
Rachel's Aunt Lesley was staying there
too. She was a respected local doctor, and
the girls had really enjoyed spending time
with her during the holiday.

"Do you think that sounds all right,

girls?" asked Aunt Lesley, looking nervous. "I feel a bit silly practising what I'll say if I win the award."

Aunt Lesley had been nominated for the Tippington Helper of the Year Award. It was a local prize that rewarded the special people in the community who had a job helping others, and the ceremony was that evening at Tippington Town Hall.

"You definitely need to have a speech ready," said Rachel. "You're bound to win!"

"I'm not so sure," said Aunt Lesley with a laugh. "You've met most of the other nominees. They're all brilliant at their jobs."

Kirsty and Rachel nodded.

"Isobel the firefighter and Colin the paramedic are wonderful," said Rachel.

"And I'm sure Mark the lifeguard is amazing," Kirsty added. "But we want *you* to win!"

Aunt Lesley smiled at them.

"I'm so pleased that I've had your company this week," she said. "You two always seem to be having fun."

Read **Lulu the Lifeguard Fairy** to find out what adventures are in store for Kirsty and Rachel!

Calling all parents, carers and teachers!
The Rainbow Magic fairies are here to help
your child enter the magical world of reading.
Whatever reading stage they are at, there's
a Rainbow Magic book for everyone!
Here is Lydia the Reading Fairy's guide to
supporting your child's journey at all levels.

Read along the Reading Rainbow!

Well done – you have completed the book!

This book was worth 1 star.

See how far you have climbed on the Reading Rainbow.
The more books you read, the more stars you can colour in
and the closer you will be to becoming a Royal Fairy!

Do you want to print your own Reading Rainbow?

1) Go to the Rainbow Magic website

2) Download and print out the poster

3) Colour in a star for every book you finish
and climb the Reading Rainbow

4) For every step up the rainbow,
you can download your very own certificate

There's all this and lots more at
rainbowmagicbooks.co.uk

You'll find activities, stories, a special newsletter
AND you can search for the fairy with your name!